TO THE MOST IMPORTANT MOTHERS IN MY LIFE:
Firstly, to the memory of my own mother, June Carter Cash,
whose unconditional love and gentle way are still within my heart.
Secondly, to my wife, Laura, whose steadfast loyalty
to her children and family I value above all else in life.

ACKNOWLEDGMENTS: I must give special thanks to my agent, Kate Etue, for the
concept, inspiration, and direction on this book. Also gracious thanks to my manager, Lou Robin;
editor Dee Ann Grand; Valerie Garfield; Rick Richter; Leyah Jensen; Jeanie Lee;
Kimberly Ainsworth; and all at Simon & Schuster who have believed in this book and been
essential to its creation. And to Marc: thank you for the vision and your commitment to it.

–J. C. C.

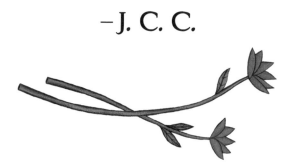

To my mom, whose love and support
I'll always hold close to my heart

– M. B.

LITTLE SIMON INSPIRATIONS
An imprint of Simon & Schuster Children's Publishing Division • 1230 Avenue of the Americas, New York, New York 10020
Text copyright © 2009 by John Carter Cash • Illustrations copyright © 2009 by Marc Burckhardt • Book design by Leyah Jensen
All rights reserved, including the right of reproduction in whole or in part in any form. • LITTLE SIMON INSPIRATIONS
is a registered trademark of Simon & Schuster, Inc., and associated colophon is a trademark of Simon & Schuster, Inc.
Manufactured in the United States of America • First Edition • 2 4 6 8 10 9 7 5 3 1
Library of Congress Cataloging-in-Publication Data: Cash, John Carter.
Momma loves her little son / by John Carter Cash ; illustrated by Marc Burckhardt. — 1st ed. • p. cm. • "Rising sun."
Summary: From the farthest shores to the deepest oceans, a mother's love for her child is without bounds.
ISBN 978-1-4169-5912-0 (hardcover : alk. paper) • [1. Stories in rhyme. 2. Mother and child—Fiction. 3. Love—Fiction.]
I. Burckhardt, Marc, 1962- ill. II. Title. • PZ8.3.C2713Mo 2009 • [E]—dc22 • 2008028373

JOHN CARTER CASH

Momma Loves Her Little Son

Illustrated by Marc Burckhardt

LITTLE SIMON INSPIRATIONS
New York London Toronto Sydney

Momma loves her little son.
There is nothing more so true.
From now until forever more,
Momma clings to you.

As far away as China,

as deep as the blue sea . . .

. . . Momma's love is
tall as a mountain,
and as strong
as a great oak tree.

Momma's love is as real as the wind,

and as bright as a rainbow.

Momma's love is as tough as a rhino's hide,

and as eager as a seed under snow.

And from the top of the tallest skyscraper,

all around the far side of the sun . . .

. . . all the way from east to west . . .

Momma loves her precious one!

Momma loves her little son,
as we count rocks and fishes.

And tell the salamanders and the toads

all our secret wishes.

Momma loves her little son,
and, oh, what fun we'll find!

We will dance across the starry skies,

together, you and I.

As true as yesterday,
and as real as right now,
when tomorrow comes,
Momma loves you more somehow.

Now the day is at its end,
we kneel to pray bedside.
Momma holds your tiny hand,
and love just grows inside.

And if you are to toss and turn,
and just can't sleep tonight . . .
Momma will come and sing to you,
and hold you safe and tight.

Momma loves her little son.
And prays you have good dreams.
And may you wake with joyous thoughts
of sunshine happy things.